törten

MURDER AND CRIME MYSTERIES FROM A BAUHAUS ESTATE

EDITED BY
NATASCHA MEUSER

törten

MURDER AND CRIME MYSTERIES FROM A BAUHAUS ESTATE

EDITED BY
NATASCHA MEUSER

CONTENT

THE TAXIDERMIST 7
ALEXANDER ZIEM / STEFAN BIEBER

AN ABERRATION OF A MALODOROUS KIND 15
BRUNO LEONARD BAUMGARDT / LIU JINXIN

THE BAUHAUS DIALOGUE 21
CHRISTIAN ALBRECHT / LUBA EMELANOW

THE SWIMMING POOL 29
SILKE KIONTKE / LENA JAEHN

THE HOUSE OF FISH SCALES 37
YVONNE HEIN / TIM REITMEIER

ORNAMENTATION AND CRIME 43
YILDIZ GÜCLÜ / ADRIEN MARVIN MATZINGER

THE SECRET ROOM 49
ISABELLE CELINE WUTTKE / THI MINH ANH

MILDENSEE 57
ANGELINA KRAETSCH / STEPHAN SCHULZE

MR WAGNER WILL NO LONGER BE VISITING 65
HENDRIK SCHULZ / LOREEN STUMPF

THE JUNKERS BEQUEST 71
MARIUS MÜLLER / ZAIXIAO WANG

1

THE TAXIDERMIST

BASED ON AN IDEA BY
ALEXANDER ZIEM / STEFAN BIEBER

THE TAXIDERMIST

Johannes Bauer was a quiet man who didn't have much to do with his neighbours. He wasn't seen to be unfriendly but just as somewhat odd. At about seven he would step out the door of his block at No. 61 to pick up his morning newspaper. He might offer a curt nod whenever a neighbour walked past him on the dead straight road but would never strike up a conversation. As a consequence very little was known about him. The only thing that was known was that Bauer had moved back from Leipzig to his hometown of Dessau in 1930, following the death of his thirty-one-year-old wife in childbirth. He appeared to have no family. In one of the few conversations he had been obliged to conduct he remarked that as a young widower the spacious Wilhelminian-era apartment where he had lived with his wife in northern Leipzig had come to seem empty and lifeless in his time of melancholy. »Instead of a family I suddenly no longer had anyone,« he had said in a rare fit of candour.

Johannes Bauer was thus deemed to be a rather desolate figure who quite understandably bemoaned his lot. Twice per week Bauer would drag his hunched frame, complete with the somewhat clumsy gait peculiar to him, across the Großring to make some purchases in the nearby Muldestrand Inn. If the wind whistled a little more strongly than usual the few remaining hairs on his head would stand awry. As a result he wore a ski-cap en route in summer and winter alike. His neighbours found something sinister about him, without being able to identify exactly why. He hardly ever had visitors, apart from some huntsmen who brought him dead animals three or four times a month, since he was a taxidermist by trade and had set up a small workshop in his cellar. He only kept in touch with his neighbour from No. 63, Hermann Gorßler, a freelance artist who also lived alone. Gorßler had dedicated his life to sculpture with moderate success, fashioning elephants from natural stone. He was reasonably well-known in Dessau for his quaint sculptures adorning the municipal park and several nearby playgrounds. Both neighbours got along quite well without talking too much and had met on two evenings each week over a number of years for a game of chess. Subsequently, however, the relationship between both men underwent a change.

This was marked by the fact that Gorßler began to use his skilful craftmanship to renovate his house; he could no longer bear colourless surfaces and clad No. 63 in exposed masonry, going on to decorate the windows with increasingly more startlingly colourful curtains. He sewed these together from pieces of fabric he had once acquired from the Bauhaus workshops during his apprenticeship, just like his chess set made of cube-shaped pieces. Shortly afterwards he converted his entrance into an odd-looking portal with brick ornamentation, also mounting coloured-glass panes on to the long row of windows. Bauer viewed the goings-on of his neighbour with some suspicion. He did not, generally speaking, like any changes to his surroundings, still less to the actual buildings of the settlement, since these changes played havoc with the harmonious uniformity he considered sacred. Bauer was a great admirer of the architect Walter Gropius. Tampering with the latter's work at one's own behest appeared an unpardonable sacrilege to him. During games of chess beneath the highly positioned cement window frames of the living room increasingly acrimonious disputes became ever more common, until Bauer finally barred his neighbour from his home.

The steel entrance door henceforth remained closed to Gorßler, who now more than ever felt emboldened to make further renovations to his house and had the appropriate materials delivered to his garden. But before Gorßler could set about these further works, he suddenly vanished. When summoned by the neighbours some weeks later the police found in the living room a farewell letter lying on the lid of the modular cabinet that served as an escritoire. In the letter the missing person stated that he intended to pursue his happiness in Hinduism and had emigrated to India. Since there seemed to be no evidence of any crime the representatives of the authorities let the matter rest.

When Johannes Bauer, the quiet taxidermist, passed away twenty-three years later alone and at home, it took weeks before officers – summoned by the neighbours – discovered the half-decayed remains of Bauer lying in the terrazzo bathtub in the kitchen. They then went on to stumble upon two elaborately stuffed human corpses in the cellar. An elderly neighbour identified one as being Hermann Gorßler. The other consisted of a heavily-pregnant woman whom the coroner estimated as being roughly thirty years old.

2

AN ABERRATION OF A MALODOROUS KIND

BASED ON AN IDEA BY
BRUNO BAUMGARDT / LIU JINXIN

04 3040

AN ABERRATION OF A MALODOROUS KIND

It was a warm, sunny Friday morning when police sergeant Enrico Krause set out on his weekly patrol across the tranquil garden settlement of Törten. His colleague Maik Hadelig, a young whippersnapper aged just twenty-one and on outdoor duty that day for the very first time, seemed visibly agitated. He was following his boss on his official-issue scooter. Krause was finding difficulty in pinpointing why the young police cadet seemed full of eager anticipation. It was not as if they were driving into the Bronx after all, but rather into a respectable neighbourhood with rows of terraced housing where any rowdy youths even knocking over a dustbin would suffice to create a scandal. Krause knew Törten well; he had been doing this job for over thirty years and had never once seen anything out of the ordinary. Over this time he had become aware that Törten itself was generally considered something special owing to its architecture. Krause himself found the area rather bleak, however. The symmetry of the housing seemed to have conferred itself upon its residents over time

such that they all looked the same age, skulked in a similarly hunched fashion through the streets and bore faces etched with the same air of resignation.
Police sergeant Krause couldn't understand why tourists would occasionally go out of their way to visit Törten and take photographs of the modest terraced housing which looked neither unique nor particularly valuable. If he were to be honest the somewhat paltry front gardens entirely bereft of underground storage facilities for their dustbins actually depressed him. This was only matched by the efforts to create something resembling beauty evident in the home-made window dressings. Krause had never set foot in any of the houses and couldn't imagine what living there would be like. Krause wound down the car window: »Let's go on foot for a few metres,« he called out to the young whippersnapper on the scooter. »A bit of a walk will do us good in this weather.«
Both men were walking in silence across the deserted Triftweg when a delivery van drove slowly past them. Out of the corner of his eye Krause noted some twitching activity taking place behind the net curtains adorning several windows. When the policemen approached house No. 17 Krause's senses were hit by a pungent chemical odour. Wait a moment. Had something happened in the building? Was it some kind of accident perhaps involving solvents? Could there be a fire

hazard? Or was it the combination of midday heat, fatigue and the bright yellow masonry paint pulling tricks on him? The young whippersnapper was by now positively fidgeting with a thirst for action – »Herr Krause, I recognise this smell from my training. We may well be dealing with a drug den hidden away in this house. Synthetic amphetamine, know what I mean.« Krause had heard about this sort of thing – but surely not here? In Törten? He shrugged his shoulders. »Very well, let's take a look. I take it you know what to do if this is the case?« To be honest, he himself didn't actually know what to do. And why did he have to stumble upon a drugs laboratory today of all days, on a colleague's first patrol of Törten? Krause called the control centre. Suspicion of a drugs offence, possible organised criminality, an unsecured crime scene. A young couple were registered at the address, everything appeared to be completely in order – nothing suspicious at all. The names conformed to those on the doorbell panel. Colleagues were en route. Krause decided to obtain access to the property. Imminent danger – it may indeed have been an accident and this putrid smell was by no means at all normal. The front door, a cheap DIY product, put up no resistance. How could people running a drug den be so careless? »If the old steel doors were still there we would definitely now have a problem,« said the young whippersnapper softly. Old steel doors? What was he talking about? Packaging materials were piled up within the hallway. Were illegal drugs now being dispatched by post?

Krause preferred not to ask. The rooms on the ground floor gave the impression of being uncluttered and clean. In the kitchen there was only an espresso machine to be found, but no Bunsen burners or flasks. The three small rooms on the first floor were obviously being used for storage. Glass jars, plastic bottles and small ampoules were lined up on wall racks. In the largest room facing the street there were three computers on a desk. In front of them lay packages bearing the inscription »Laboratory Equipment«. Krause inhaled deeply.

Drug trafficking in Dessau after all, evidently some big shot running their own mail order business, perhaps internationally. »What do you think?« he asked his young colleague who simply shrugged his shoulders. »I don't think we're dealing with drugs here,« he said. Eh? No drugs? Krause shook his head irritably. The laboratory equipment, the computers, the glass jars – was that not enough to justify raising initial suspicions? And wasn't it the case that this pungent smell was totally synthetic and had a somewhat befuddling effect? »Here, take a look.« Krause stared at the Smartphone. »That's a website,« said the whippersnapper, »for Hen House Beauty, based in Törten. They manufacture beauty products.« Krause stared in amazement again. Who knew all the things Törten had to offer!

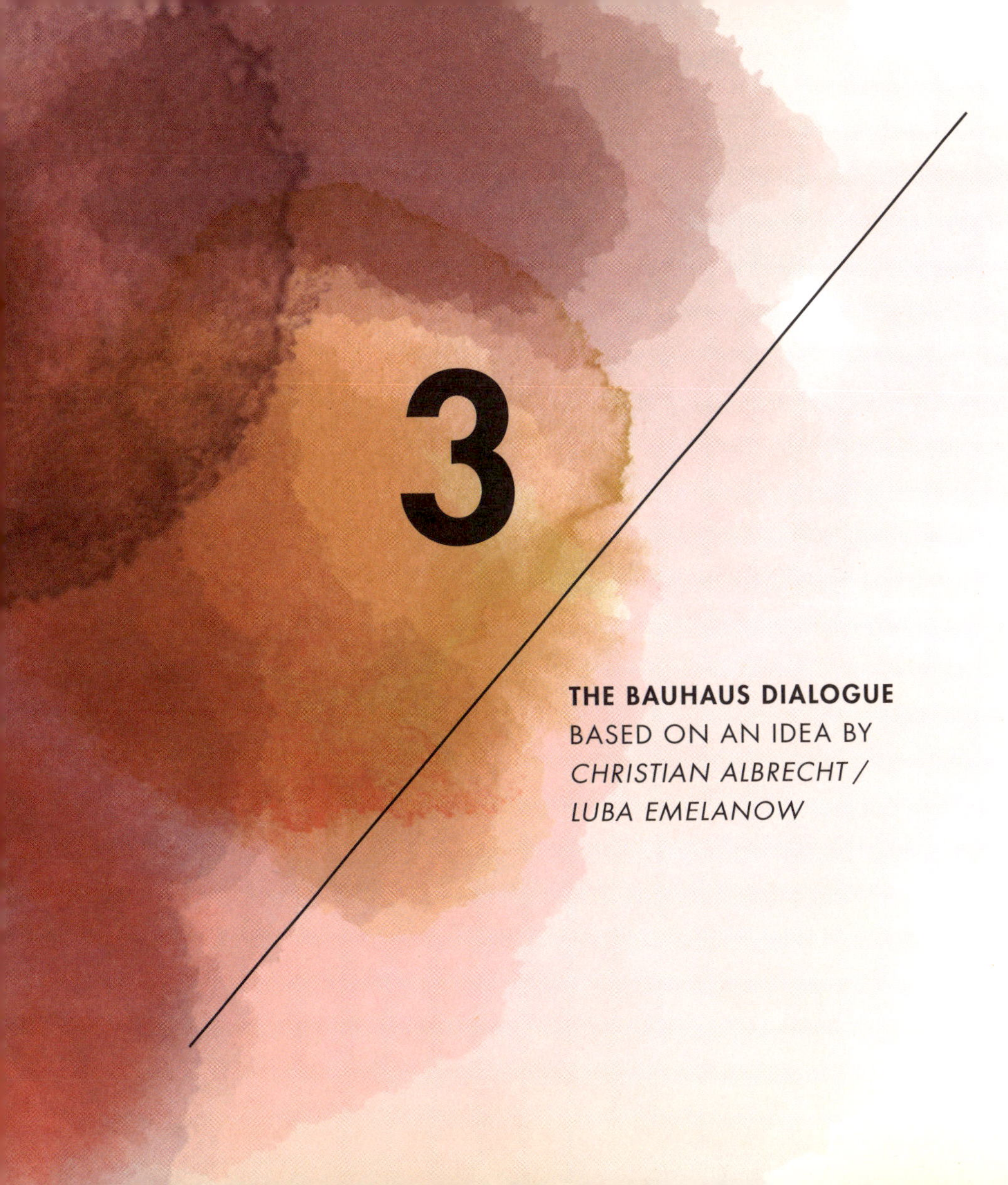

3

THE BAUHAUS DIALOGUE

BASED ON AN IDEA BY
CHRISTIAN ALBRECHT /
LUBA EMELANOW

BAUHAUS

THE BAUHAUS DIALOGUE

Here, take a look, this is supposed to be outstanding architecture. World famous. Ha! I'll tell you what it is – it's a terraced house in Dessau-Törten, in other words not exactly Beverly Hills if you ask me. Seventy-five square metres of living space over two floors with a partial cellar and a garden. Nothing special at all. You will, of course, need some good ideas and the right materials to make something of it. However that's what I'm here for. Look, here we have the kitchen on the ground floor. Entirely stupid if you ask me. A bathtub right next to the washing-up sink – what good is that to anyone? My wife doesn't want it – we already have a dishwasher. But to try and rip it out, crikey, what an infernal job that would be! Maybe we could use it to keep carp in? Or plant it up with something? It has to be said though it's still in good shape, the old tub. And it's not everyone who has one of those. The light terrazzo flooring is not bad, I admit, although the colour is not in keeping with the new kitchen. Maybe we could lay a couple of vinyl tiles on top to cover it up?

Nope? Very well then, you're the expert. And you genuinely like those rather dilapidated-looking kitchen cabinets, do you? They are a bit of a sorry sight – far too plain for us. We've already decided upon something new – dark blue with a mirror finish, real fancy. That should look really, really nice later. Well now it's a pity the idea of knocking through into the living room will come to nothing since that tub and the old sink unit are in the way. But thank goodness we still have the original opening as we're intending to install a sliding glass door there. Do you think that'll look nice? Yes, it was my idea.

We would have liked to convert the living room window facing the street in order to create a panoramic outlook, but were refused permission. No matter – we'll turn it into a cosy parlour. But we definitely need a new window, triple-glazed would be best. Do you have anything on offer? Plastic, you say? Frankly, for my part the main thing is that it doesn't come in too expensive.

Old buildings are always good for surprises – who knows what kind of people would have lived there in former times? You could still see the name written on the doorbell panel, probably somebody important at the Bauhaus. Imagine someone like that being forced to live in such a dive? Well, it was his granddaughter who sold us the house. Strange old dear, I must say. And do you know what – one room on the upper

floor is locked and we haven't got a key that fits. A bit weird, don't you think? My wife says she can sometimes hear noises at night coming from that room, but I think she's just going nuts because the building work is going so slowly and we're still sleeping on inflatable mattresses. Yes yes, you're quite right, there is in fact plenty of space upstairs – there are three rooms there. The large bedroom facing onto the street and two small ones – one of which, as I have said, is locked. Who knows what junk is piled up in there? I will attend to it once the other rooms are finished. We are keen at all costs to lay laminate flooring. Perhaps birch, that'd be nice and bright. Ah yes, the walls – we haven't discussed those yet. We'll need to get some nice wallpaper put up. There's just so much to choose from that'll look fantastic. From Glöckler, you say? Oh no, that would cost far too much for me.
Tell me about the latest trends then – I don't mind lining paper, but my wife always goes for something extravagant. Clean off the plaster and give it a smooth finishing coat? Who's going to pick up the bill for that then? No, no my good man, trends are all well and good, but I'm after something reasonable rather than bare-looking walls. Look, a richly textured wallpaper like that could create a really upmarket look. Perhaps in a soft grey colour? I'll take a sample away with me. But to get back to that locked room. It really is a bit

spooky, since it's been fitted with a professional safety lock and we haven't even been able to get the door open using force. The granddaughter says she doesn't remember where the key is. She has supposedly never been inside that room, can you imagine that? She has lived in the house for seventy years! And the lock is evidently Westware, so it must have been installed sometime after 1990. Look, you can see from the plans that it is simply a small room with just enough space for a bed, a table, a chair and a wardrobe. Well, when we're finished insulating the facade we'll break the door down. What did you say, how many square metres of insulating material do we need? Goodness, that's going to cost a packet!

Ah, then there's also the old livestock pen in the garden to consider. We still don't know quite what to do with it – there's so much stuff inside and it smells of damp and mould too. The rain has been getting in to it for ages. Those wooden boxes are past their best, so we'll arrange for them to be picked up and taken away. What's inside them? Why, you are funny – how should I know? It says »Amber Room« on them. But I haven't found any amber in any of the rooms. Such nonsense!

4

THE SWIMMING POOL

BASED ON AN IDEA BY
SILKE KIONTKE / LENA JAEHN

BOOKBOX

THE SWIMMING POOL

I'll get some peace soon, Marianne Frick is thinking as the men from the removal service put the last boxes down. She gives them an appropriate tip, sinks down on to the couch and says to her daughter Petra, »At last we've made it to our new very own domain.« The four-year-old looks around the plain square-shaped living room somewhat apprehensively, then turns her gaze – in order to evade that of her mother – towards the steel window spanning almost the width of the room. It is so high up that from her perspective she can see nothing but a leafless bonsai tree and the grey rain-streaked sky above Törten. »I want to go back home to Papa,« says Petra. »Oh, sweetheart,« replies her mother, »Just think about summer when we'll have a swimming pool in the garden.« Marianne had promised her daughter one in order to make the move more palatable. The recent few months had been sheer agony for Marianne. After her husband Paul had lost his job at the sugar refinery in Dessau he had begun drinking beer as soon as he got up – which was towards midday. Although he

spent the entire day at home he never helped with the household chores. By night at the amusement arcade he would fritter away the small inheritance recently bequeathed to Marianne by her father. One day, when the quarrelling escalated yet again he slapped Marianne in the face right in front of Petra. Although Paul did subsequently act sheepish and did vacuum the apartment every once in a while, Marianne's mind had nevertheless been made up.

She began studying Property for Sale advertisements within the local news section of the Mitteldeutsche newspaper. Marianne dreamt of having a little house for Petra and herself. She had thought she could manage this using the inheritance and her income as a clerical assistant within the municipality. Yet everything she found proved to be beyond her means. At the end of October a colleague gave her a tip-off. »The pool attendant's house is going to compulsory auction in two weeks,« he said. The latter had purportedly left his wife, who now wanted to get rid of the house. Like everybody else in Dessau, Marianne knew the story. The man had supposedly won a huge sum of money on the lottery and had now carved out a pleasant life for himself abroad. It was said that he had moved to Bali. Sun, sea and beautiful women had always been his preferred choices. Marianne didn't hesitate long when it came to the auction. She was neither

hesitant nor shy to act; the house pleased her, there was only one other bidder and she was able to muster the necessary price of 80,000 deutschmarks. The hammer fell and Marianne was proud of her courage. In the ensuing weeks prior to the move she made plans as to how she was going to furnish the place. The clean lines of the house sat happily with her liking for all things simple and practical. She liked the central location of the kitchen where, irrespective of whether she was spending time in the living room or the garden, she could keep an eye on Petra playing. Marianne had already ordered a comfortable reclining chair complete with side table for the roof terrace and fondly imagined how she would lie there and read as Petra slumbered at night indirectly opposite in the largest of the three rooms on the upper storey. But most of all she was looking forward to her own bedroom which she would have all to herself. This lay alongside the room leading to the roof terrace which she intended to furnish as a dressing room and was more or less square in shape. Marianne spent the following weeks furnishing the house. Since she had been forced to leave a lot behind and wanted to save money she roamed flea markets far and wide as well as used furniture salesrooms so that, little by little, the house eventually filled up. With most of this attended to shortly before the end of Spring Marianne turned her attention to the large garden.

Half a dozen apple and pear trees could be found in full bud on the hindmost periphery of the 75 m long – but merely 5.9 m wide – strip of greenery. In front you could see previously uncultivated vegetable patches. The last owners had converted the former livestock pen into a pretty garden hut. A somewhat dilapidated climbing frame was to be found on the large adjoining meadowland. Marianne set to with the mowing and weeding, washing down the brick-paved terrace and applying a coat of blue paint to the concrete fence posts demarcating the neighbouring property. She also replaced the three rusty cables tightened at different heights.
»And where do you want your little swimming pool to go?« she asks her daughter one day when everything had been seen to. Petra takes a look around and points to a shady spot next to two enormous rhododendron bushes. A few days later a small digger judders its way along the access route and enters the garden through the rear gate. Marianne has marked off the 3 m by 4 m area into which the pool is to be subsequently embedded. The shovel burrows into the ground but after just a few minutes the operator stops work saying he's encountered two blue bin liners at a depth of roughly 90 cm. The discovery makes international headlines. The wife of the pool attendant will subsequently testify before the Court:
»I didn't want to have to share him with ever more women.«

5

THE HOUSE OF FISH SCALES

BASED ON AN IDEA BY

YVONNE HEIN /

TIM REITMEIER

THE HOUSE OF FISH SCALES

We should have guessed, said the neighbours subsequently. The strange cladding of the house in fish skin and the fish tank in the window if nothing else. Yes, they thought, there had been signs that there was something amiss with Triemer. But a tale like that? Nobody was quite sure precisely when Triemer had arrived in Törten. The old Schweigert woman at Number 14 was resolute in insisting that he had originally moved in with his wife but over the years it had only ever been Triemer they had seen out and about. He was a quiet, inconspicuous fellow whom no one could properly describe. Neither tall nor short, not slim but not plump, with hair of a nondescript colour and somehow seemingly ageless. In the morning he would leave the small terraced house shortly after seven and would return in the early hours of the evening, although whether he was holding down a steady job – as everyone had believed – was highly doubtful following events. In Törten it was inconceivable for one person to be different from the others. Just as the terraced houses all looked alike, so too their occupants seemed to be strangely uniform. Their domestic lives took place within identical rooms: the kitchen and living room on the ground floor, the bathroom, bedrooms and children's room on the first. Each semi-detached house was reflected in minute detail in that next door, rendering neighbours identical twins in terms of residence.

Accordingly, Triemer's renovation of his facade prompted much tongue-wagging. He started by gradually replacing the plain plaster finish with a dark, serried layer of scales that from a distance looked like slate but which would glisten when it rained, seeming to set the small house in motion. Mrs Libkovsky from next door – while emphasising that it certainly was none of her business – nevertheless complained to old Schweigert about the peculiar smell emanating from the new facade. No doubt some cheap product from China. Mrs Libkovsky did not want to point any fingers, but worried about possible harmful substances and the value of her half of the house. And it was not only old Schweigert who thoroughly agreed with her. Triemer himself did not comment. Only when his living room window began to glow at night did Mrs Libkovsky ring at his door. She did not want to be intrusive, she said affably, but someone had evidently forgotten to switch off the light in the living room in the evening. She was no longer slept so well and had noticed it. Ultimately electricity was becoming more and more expensive, wouldn't he agree? She attempted to look past him into the house from which splashing noises were drifting out. Triemer thanked her and closed the door. Mrs Libkovsky seized her opportunity and stole a look at the coldly luminous living room window, peering directly into a red eye belonging to a fish which slipped into view then swam along unperturbed, disappearing into murky greenish depths. She stood still, as if frozen.

A fish tank within the living room window? Was that even permitted? Mrs Libkovsky shook her head. This Triemer was truly a most peculiar person. And what kind of fish were those anyway? She had never seen such large ones before – not in a fish tank in any event.

Half amused, half nauseated she told old Schweigert about Triemer's hobby and did not concern herself with it any further. Rather, she fretted over her cat which had vanished a few days ago and wasn't responding to enticing tones or the specially cooked goulash within the bowl on the terrace. Mrs Libkovsky decided to ask Triemer – he must have seen the cat. After all, they shared the garden and terrace to a certain extent. Her inconspicuous neighbour responded surprisingly abruptly and evasively. A cat? What cat? Never laid eyes upon it.

Have a nice evening! He slammed the door in Mrs Libkovsky's face. A few days later, when the cat had still not resurfaced, she spotted a placard on the street. A small dog had gone missing, last seen on Damaschkestraße. Once it was dark enough at night Mrs Libkovsky walked softly to the fish tank within the window. It took a while before one of the large fishes appeared. By torch light Mrs Libkovsky compared the illustration within the open book with that which swam before her. She remembered her cat and the missing puppy from Damaschkestraße and also Triemer's wife, whom nobody had ever seen before apart from old Schweigert. She then closely regarded the obscure fish with the red eyes once more.
Pygocentrus nattereri, popularly known as a piranha.
A pet in Törten.

6

ORNAMENTATION AND CRIME

BASED ON AN IDEA BY

YILDIZ GÜCLÜ /

ADRIEN MARVIN MATZINGER

DIE
BÜHN
BAUHAUSBÜCHER
4

ORNAMENTATION AND CRIME

Fred was considered a bit of a lone wolf among his neighbours. Unlike the other children in Törten he didn't attend the local secondary school, but rather a boarding school in Lutherstadt Wittenberg. The Year 9 pupil only came home at weekends and during holidays. He would then stay in his room and read. Although he obtained high marks, Fred was no swot; learning simply came easy to him. His style of clothing was somewhat unusual – Fred was permanently dressed in a black suit with a polo-neck jumper of the same colour underneath. His hair was short, closely shaven. His parents adopted a hands-off approach with him – possibly out of a free-spirited disposition, but primarily since they were far too preoccupied with themselves.

Fred's mother described herself as a poet, although for the most part she seemed to pour her energy into her Kabbala studies. His father, an engineer in the atomic industry under the communists, lost his job with the fall of the Berlin Wall and now supported the family as a freelance software engineer. In his spare time he would observe the stars from the large roof terrace of his study. The two did not talk much which is why they almost never quarrelled.

Only seldom did they enter Fred's room, the largest of three on the upper storey. The boy found this just as well, since this meant he could pursue undisturbed his penchant for the art and architecture of the Bauhaus school. Prints by Klee, Itten, Kandinsky and Schlemmer hung on the wall to the right of the window within Fred's room; on the left were photographs by Albers, Feininger, Moholy-Nagy and Peterhans. He had pigeon-holed into his large bookcase monographs on artists and architects alongside illustrated books on their works and buildings as well as dozens of exhibition catalogues – all placed according to a strictly observed order. The boy had acquired two or three of these second-hand with his pocket money, although he owed the vast majority of his treasure trove to his neighbour. Fred visited the unmarried daughter (from his second marriage) of the Bauhaus director – who had died in the 1950s – as often as her state of health permitted. The old woman was still mentally alert despite her advanced years although she often suffered from painful episodes owing to her multiple sclerosis, and would proceed to stay in bed for days on end. In good times, however, Fred and Mrs M. would sit together over tea and pastries during seemingly never-ending afternoons, chatting about the illustriousness of the Bauhaus school, the fatherly director of the Bauhaus and the history of Törten housing estate.

Fred painstakingly took copious notes in his large notebook. The fact that there was no place on earth more beautiful than the living room and kitchen of Mrs M. was not solely owing to the woman herself and her seemingly boundless knowledge. The furnishing of the house, with its furniture and installations preserved in the original style, filled the boy with at least as much enthusiasm. If Fred stood in front of the steel entrance door and pressed the button on the doorbell panel from Messing, he could hear how the electric bell system by Siemens-Schuckert would ring out in the hallway. He stumbled upon the cabinet assembled from individual cubes by Marcel Breuer within the living room and a shelf unit by the same designer on the wall facing the kitchen, both dating back to the year 1926. The original furnishings of the living room – the sewing table, chairs, stools – were just as well preserved as the sink and the bathtub made of terrazzo within the kitchen. Even the old Gaco water heater was still hanging on the wall. Fred felt as if he were in paradise.

One late afternoon, however, a crack appeared in Fred's idyll. Initially everything was the same as always. Mrs M. chatted about old times, her memories of Walter Gropius, the amusing games with the young Andreas in the Feiningers' garden and the relocation of the School from Weimar to Dessau. Then the neighbour fell silent. Since she appeared anxious, Fred asked what the matter was. Hesitantly she admitted to being worried. Her inheritance was more or less depleted and her pension was too small to live on. She didn't want to part with the furniture and the house but, since she had in her possession something amounting to a sensation which would bring in a lot of money, she was going to sell that. Nevertheless, it meant that her father's reputation would be ruined after it. Fred was baffled and continued to speculate over what it might be, remaining completely in the dark. Finally Mrs M. went to the cabinet by Marcel Breuer, opened the door of the largest cube with its French polish and unearthed a dusty art portfolio which she laid upon the living room table. »Please,« she said. With jittery hands, Fred opened the folder, flipped the cover open and froze: it was a design for a baroque villa laden with ornamentation, signed by Mr M. »Father always privately hated the Bauhaus aesthetic,« said his daughter. Now everyone would know about it. Inside Fred's head his world was caving in, but he acted swiftly. Without further hesitation, he pressed the cushion featuring a pattern designed by Anni Albers into his neighbour's face as she cowered on her armchair – until she stopped breathing. Then he went home. Two days later the doctor recorded »coronary failure« on the death certificate. There was only one beneficiary named in the Will. And that was Fred.

7

THE SECRET ROOM
BASED ON AN IDEA BY
ISABELLE CELINE WUTTKE / THI MINH ANH

THE SECRET ROOM

It was only with some reluctance that Klaus Harnisch had entered into matrimony with Eva Lohmann. The pair had met in the mid-1990s at Bielefeld University of Applied Sciences. Klaus pursued his studies with moderate aptitude and interest in equal measure and was almost grateful when the ambitious Eva took a liking to him. Although Klaus found the sallow diabetic woman somewhat insipid, he surrendered to her less than bountiful femininity one evening, fuelled by wine. When Eva broke it to him towards the end of the last semester that a joint future was imminent with the words, »I'm pregnant,« he acquiesced, albeit with a heavy heart.

The pair moved to the eastern sector following the wedding, since both had found employment at the Förch firm in Dessau. They found a small unfussy house in the Törten garden settlement which was in keeping with Eva's appreciation of the neatly laid-out, clinical tastes of the petty bourgeois. She liked the rhythmic structuring of the facades, running almost in belt-like fashion, as well as the small porches, alongside

which recessed steel entry doors safeguarded the familial security lying behind. »We're going to live here,« said Eva.
The first weeks elapsed and were taken up with the furnishing of the small house. They selected the room on the upper storey overlooking the garden for the child, immediately opposite the stairs, and painted it light pink in anticipation of a girl. »This will please Martina,« thought Eva to herself – without having discussed her choice of name with Klaus.
As later became all too apparent, Klaus proved to be just as dispassionate in this matter as he was towards his daughter herself. Martina was the spitting image of her mother, albeit appearing even paler within the pinkish hues of her bedroom.
Eva was constantly preoccupied with imposing order. She took a particular shine to the closet above the double-L shaped stair. This reached to ceiling height and offered plenty of storage space without encroaching on the living space. She also liked the central location of the kitchen on the ground floor which she referred to as the »distribution room« owing to its five doors, one of which descended into the cellar with its walls of slag cement.
One Saturday Eva decided to do a bit of tidying up down there. Klaus was at home and she reckoned he would hear Martina if she woke up. She went down the steel staircase and set about putting the contents of the remaining removal

boxes up on to shelves which the previous owner had left behind. Martina woke up in less than half an hour and Klaus went down to the cellar in order to let her mother know so she could attend to her. Yet Eva was nowhere to be seen within a room which was scarcely the width of the hallway. While Klaus was pondering whether she had perhaps left the cellar and gone upstairs, he heard a faint scraping sound from behind the shelving. He held his breath in order to be able to listen in better and then heard a whimpering sound alongside the disheartened scraping noises. Klaus allowed himself a tacit smile. Not normally a man of action, he was fast on his feet now. He left the cellar, glanced at the kitchen clock and knew that without insulin in another two hours Eva would be dead. He took the meuling Martina into his arms, whereupon she promptly ratcheted up the level of her wailing and called out for her mother with a weak voice. »Mummy's gone and will never come back,« said Klaus in a gleeful singsong voice, setting out for a long stroll with Martina in the pushchair. Contrary to his usual practice he exchanged a word outside with a neighbour in order to strengthen his alibi. »Your new blinds look very nice, Mr Möllner,« he yelled over, alluding to the colour which had been imposed on the windows next door – and then he wandered off with the wailing Martina. Back home, he went down into the cellar once more.

The whimpering had fallen silent; the scraping noises could no longer be heard. He shook the shelf – gently at first, then more violently. Nothing moved. Klaus took a closer look and discovered a small matt silver lever. When he lifted this up a narrow steel door to which the left part of the furniture was attached swung open. A lifeless Eva cowered within the opening behind it. His heart leapt with relief. His elation continued to grow when he stepped closer. An old suitcase filled to the brim with 100 dollar bundled up banknotes lay in the rear right corner. Once more Klaus was fast on his feet.
He stuffed the suitcase into the closet above the stairs and phoned an ambulance. »Obviously she must have accidentally locked herself in, couldn't get out and was therefore unable to inject herself with insulin,« said Klaus in his statement to the young policewoman. »I myself had gone for a stroll with my child. My neighbour Mr Möllner can attest to that,« he added, insinuating emotional closure. The police dropped investigations following further lines of questioning. Klaus packed the suitcase containing the money into the car, handed his daughter over to a children's home on the road to Hamburg and boarded a cruise liner to Brazil, where he promptly proceeded to move into a bungalow designed by Oscar Niemeyer.

8

MILDENSEE

BASED ON AN IDEA BY

ANGELINA KRAETSCH / STEPHAN SCHULZE

MILDENSEE

Nobody within the settlement fully understood why the brothers Torsten and Bernd Junkers had never exchanged a single word for seventeen years. The more elderly neighbours recalled how they were inseparable as children and constantly spent their days together. Perhaps they clung to one another all the more because their little sister had drowned in the outdoor swimming pool in Mildensee at the time. Such is life. Since Torsten, the elder brother, had had to repeat one year, they even began their apprenticeship at the dockyard in Roßlau at the same time. There both brothers fell in love with the Krause twins from the records office shortly prior to their apprenticeship examinations. The girls were as alike as two peas in a pod. Torsten settled on the vivacious Karin, whereas Bernd's heart belonged to the more subdued Johanna. When some years later the brothers moved from the parental home at Kleinring into two adjacent houses at Mittelring – each with a master craftman's diploma under his belt – their fortunes seemed to be secured.

Together both pairs of newlyweds set about renovating the somewhat down-at-heel buildings. There was certainly enough to be done – moisture had penetrated the structure through the leaky flat roofs and had soaked the insulation put in by the previous owner. The previously whitewashed final rendering was crumbling in parts as a consequence of the dilapidated brickwork and rust had taken hold in several places. Several windows were blocked up and the garden had run to seed. The Junkers brothers, however, knew how to muck in so that both small houses were quite respectable after just a few months. They did not necessarily show much consideration for the history of the buildings though. They probably knew about the Bauhaus, since they had bought the bulk of the materials needed – as well as windows, doors, fittings and ceramics for the bathrooms – at the local building supplies merchant. The name Walter Gropius on the other hand didn't mean a thing to them. The front doors made of Wood's metal ended up in the skip without much ado, along with the window panes featuring Luxfer prismatic glass, the Junkers bathtub of spare design, the Chörtner water heater and the Oranier kitchen stove. The building supplies merchant was able to supply cost-effective replacements for these too. As summer drew to a close, both houses were in good shape: Torsten's gleamed white, Bernd's

yellow. No sooner was the paint dry than the Junkers brothers invited all the neighbours to a big garden party.
Rumour has it among those in attendance that the seeds of the rupture between Torsten and Bernd were sown that evening, although nobody knew the full facts . If one of the brothers was sitting at the bar in Sietö-Fässchen in the late hours with neighbours from the settlement, the men occasionally tried to get to the bottom of the issue. Yet no matter how much alcohol the brothers consumed, they immediately fell silent when the subject of the dispute was broached. They also never encountered each other in the pub. As the neighbours had established for quite some time, the even days belonged to Torsten and the odd ones to Bernd. They also put in different shifts at the dockyard, without exception.
When they could no longer bear this deep-rooted animosity between the brothers, the Krause twins left their husbands. Both brothers had demanded loyalty from their wives and barred them from all contact with each other. But blood is thicker than water and the sisters became as thick as thieves. Once, after they had secretly met in Vockerode, Katrin let something slip. Torsten became enraged and asked his wife whether Johanna had been telling her something about him. Katrin didn't understand what he was getting at.
He responded to her query with a simple »No matter.«

Then he went to Sietö-Fässchen and, as often happened, came home late, drunk. Eight months later the sisters moved in together, sharing a flat in Görlitz.

That might have been the end of the matter and nobody in Törten would ever have learned what happened on the evening of the garden party. Except that one of the neighbours, Werner Kramer, with whom the twins had been in the same class at school, met the rather reserved Johanna two years later at the funeral of their old class teacher. Since Katrin had come down with some ailment, Johanna came alone. Walter had doted upon Johanna before and invited her over for dinner after the burial. They spoke about old times, the deceased teacher and, of course, the settlement. Since the flattery of her old admirer pleased Johanna, she even gave her assent to a second bottle of red wine.

Time flew by and Johanna had already started feeling the worse for wear when the conversation eventually turned to the dispute between the brothers. Initially Joanna hummed and hawed and dwelt on vague phrases – an old family affair, completely tragic, a confession on the evening of the party. But Werner was persistent. Later Werner was unable to state for certain whether at some point she became too tired to continue offering resistance, or whether she simply wanted to get the matter off her chest, but when the final dregs were all that remained in her wineglass Johanna came out with it: »Torsten pushed their little sister from the diving platform during a night-time excursion. This secret will bind the brothers together forever.«

9

MR WAGNER WILL NO LONGER BE VISITING

BASED ON AN IDEA BY

HENDRIK SCHULZ / LOREEN STUMPF

DE P 961

MR WAGNER WILL NO LONGER BE VISITING

I didn't mean it. Honestly. It was not at all clear to me that I had to ask the building heritage authorities – or that building heritage authorities in charge of my house even actually existed. Seriously? I'm not exactly living in Sanssouci! Who would ever have thought that a – how did you put it – a curator is responsible for these shacks? And hand on heart – there are enough houses around here which look just like mine prior to the renovation. I genuinely fail to understand why Mr Wagner is kicking up such a fuss. After all, I am the owner and I can do whatever I like with my property – that is written into constitutional law. Mr Wagner or the building heritage authorities cannot talk me out of it if I wish to brighten up my house! It's not as if I've painted it pink. And let me tell you something else – the neighbours have all confirmed to me that the new facade with the clinker brick looks a lot better than that dreary white plaster. I grew up in a prefab housing estate, you know. Every house looked identical there.

As a child I often got lost on my way home from school because I would confuse streets and buildings. Even the smell was the same wherever you went! This was particularly distressing when I hadn't yet learned to read. How many times did I stand there howling in front of an entrance because the key did not fit, although everything was exactly the same as at home – the colours, the doorbell panels, the pushchairs in the corridor, simply everything! Those who have grown up with it haven't got a good word to say about this uniformity, irrespective of the Bauhaus.
And then there's the tourists! That's been going on for years. We sometimes get them in coachloads and always at the weekend – with their frantic photographing of each and everything around here. There's nothing to see here. Do these people drive to the prefab buildings in Muldeauen too I wonder? I just can't understand the attraction of Törten for tourists. Or maybe they consider the Neumann's house next door to be a landmark sight worth seeing? Those people have actually covered over their whole front garden with gravel. Old Mr Neumann mentioned something about a slipped disc, but I say it's just sheer laziness. My wife practically breaks her back planting and weeding so that things look a little more pleasing, and then Neumann next door goes and dumps gravel right next to it right in front of the building.

The building heritage authorities could intervene volubly here, but no – they only appear when I add some cladding to my facade. You ought to have seen this Wagner fellow and how he got all hot under the collar! And then we had that odd couple! Tourists, of course – constantly strolling around and always acting as if they know it all. They had a book with them containing old photos from former times. They strolled casually over as Wagner was just about to take a photograph of me standing with my mason's trowel on the scaffold. He might well have been trying to say that he was simply concerned about alterations to the house but I'm no fool. That the stone then struck him in such an unfortunate manner – goodness me, I was immediately greatly upset. Wagner hadn't looked quite so fragile at the time.

He was more robust in the event than that scrawny tourist couple with the thick book. What a frenzied outburst that woman erupted into! I think she was more worried about the facade than Wagner lying there bleeding. Well, I myself grew increasingly enraged at her hysterical screaming. Of course, I fully acknowledge that I shouldn't have lunged out with the trowel. My wife phoned for an ambulance immediately. The girl didn't have to be hospitalised – it was merely a laceration. Can you imagine it? Her boyfriend had in the meantime quite calmly photographed my house and was rambling on

about some detail or other. When I told him that the old doors and windows were in the shed he could hardly contain himself. He wasn't the slightest bit interested in my new brick facade. I had always thought that the tourists would be drawn to it, like Wagner. Well, he'll no longer be paying a visit.
Am I under arrest now?

10

THE JUNKERS BEQUEST

BASED ON AN IDEA BY

MARIUS MÜLLER /

ZAIXIAO WANG

THE JUNKERS BEQUEST

Johannes Hügel had never been very close to his grandfather Wilhelm. For as long as he could remember Grandpa Wilhelm had lived alone in a small cottage in Törten, a Bauhaus settlement on the other side of town. He used to work at Junkers. In 1936 he completed an apprenticeship there as a young man in order to train for the trade of tailor and upholsterer. All the time he was upholstering aircraft seats he would be dreaming about taking to the skies himself. This was never to come about, however, since he had a bad leg and was ineligible for military service. Grandpa Wilhelm liked his work and even somewhat lamented the end of the war, especially since the Junkers factory closed down in Dessau in 1951 and the firm moved to Munich. Thereafter he worked with the State-run body for the production of railway carriages, making up seats for the underground trains in Berlin and Buenos Aires – but it wasn't the same. His passion lay with flying. Johannes Hügel was aware of all this when he moved into his grandfather's little house with Angelika, his fiancée, in 1997.

The recently deceased grandfather Wilhelm had bequeathed it to his only grandson. Initially Johannes contemplated putting it up for sale, but Angelika, who had just started a course researching the Bauhaus archives, went into raptures at the prospect of being able to move in to a house within the settlement built by Walter Gropius. Since Johannes could never resist giving Angelika the least little thing she ever wanted he consented, despite his misgivings.
These misgivings primarily related to the condition of the house which grandfather Wilhelm had remodelled in keeping with his evidently very unique taste, unfettered by any awareness of architectural history. He hadn't bothered too much about adopting a thorough approach to carrying out his tasks. It was with considerable delight that the couple identified the original bound-wood screed beneath the carpeting laid by grandfather Wilhelm in his younger years. And the walls which had been smoothly plastered with lime mortar – to which the very well-preserved casein paint continued to cling – resurfaced from behind the fibreglass wallpaper. When Angelika eventually brought to light the precast on-site concrete joints from behind the Styrofoam ceiling panels, Johannes knew that they were well on track to creating a lovely home. The couple spent weeks and months decluttering the house and relieving it of ornamental deadweight. With the exception of a few

family photographs and the beautiful old sewing machine upon which grandfather Wilhelm had worked on his various tasks day-in-day-out right up until shortly before his death, Johannes got rid of everything. He was somewhat unnerved, however, by a batch of carefully cut-out newspaper reports - all of which related to lost pets from the nearby and surrounding neighbourhood. He certainly saw no convincing reason to keep on holding on to useless things solely to suit the whims of some elderly people.

Working on the basis of the cellar and the entrance area – enlarged by contrast with the first housing model constructed in 1926 – Angelika identified her new abode as Type Sietö 1.2, built in 1927. Given that only each second fire wall appeared on the facade in her row of houses, she spotted the altered structural system compared with the original and felt herself quite vindicated in her appraisal. Angelika thus began to refurbish the rooms in keeping with the old templates she had discovered within the Bauhaus archives, placing special emphasis upon the colour scheme. She got hold of source materials via old contacts of her father – a former middle-ranking bigshot with the Stasi – who reproduced the original colours for her. She affectionately varnished the door leaves and walls within the hallway in a shade of light grey, painting the door frames, the steel profile of the

partition walls on the terrace and the exterior of the kitchen window black. She furnished the interior with white oil-based paint, alternatively painting the wall and ceiling panelling in different colours – the ceilings in each room on the upper storey in alternating vibrant colours, the walls in a light grey distemper, the same colour for the walls on the ground floor and a uniform light yellow for the ceilings. When finally everything gleamed in fresh paint, the couple turned their attention to the highly pungent cellar. They had so far failed to pay close heed to the dimly lit rooms. Perhaps for that reason the large white plastic curtain hadn't actually caught their eye. This curtain, in terms of colour, scarcely set itself apart from the walls plastered with the lime-based mixture and, burdened with lead weights at the seams, did seem to droop heavily. When Johannes swept it aside, the smell became staggering. At first he didn't know what lay before him. It seemed to be some kind of huge bird, albeit without feathers. Both stepped closer. Johannes switched on the small flashlight on his bunch of keys. They then did recognise what lay in front of them – a historically accurate aircraft resembling the Derwitz machine produced by Otto Lilienthal. Johannes seized one of the wings and touched the surface held together by countless seams. He whispered to Angelika in the semi-darkness: animal skins.

For some considerable time I have been uneasy with the view of Törten as an architectural phenomenon. This gave me the idea of embarking upon an experiment – my students would approach buildings of historic significance in Dessau within the context of narrative. In so doing they would be able to experience architectural history from a completely different perspective – namely that offered by the framework of a fictional account created by themselves. In this manner students from different cultural backgrounds would arrive at a deeper understanding of the building typology of modular housing.
The Törten Project: Murder and Crime Mysteries from a Bauhaus Estate takes readers beyond the chaste white facades of the world-renowned Bauhaus settlement. Students at the Anhalt University of Applied Sciences produced and developed ideas for murder and crime mysteries in order to shed new light on the estate of terraced housing completed by Walter Gropius in 1928. This gave rise to quirky narratives about mysterious entanglements, morbid secrets and grisly intrigues – albeit all fictional accounts! What is notable about this method of teaching architecture is its attempt to adopt innovative approaches in the dissemination of knowledge. If we succeed in creating enthusiasm among readers beyond academic circles for this experiment, we will have achieved our objective.

Natascha Meuser

The Deutsche Nationalbibliothek lists this publication in the *Deutsche Nationalbibliografie;* detailed bibliographic data are available online at http://dnb.d-nb.de.

ISBN 978-3-86922-719-1

Translation
Clarice Knowles

Illustrations
Natascha Meuser

Design
Nicole Wolf

Printing
L&C Printing Group, Krakow
www.lcprinting.eu